Daddy Adventure Day

Dave Keane

ILLUSTRATED BY
Sue Ramá

PHILOMEL BOOKS • An Imprint of Penguin Group (USA) Inc.

Today is my Daddy Adventure Day.
I'm up and dressed early.
    For today's Daddy Adventure Day,
my daddy is taking me to my first
baseball game.

"It's only 4:15 in the morning," Daddy mumbles.

While I wait for him to finish sleeping, I roll his old baseballs down the stairs. *Thump-thump! Thump-thump!* I don't know how he can sleep on such an exciting day.

When a baseball bounces all the way into the living room and knocks over a lamp, Daddy finally gets out of bed.

Daddy Adventure Days are always full of surprises.

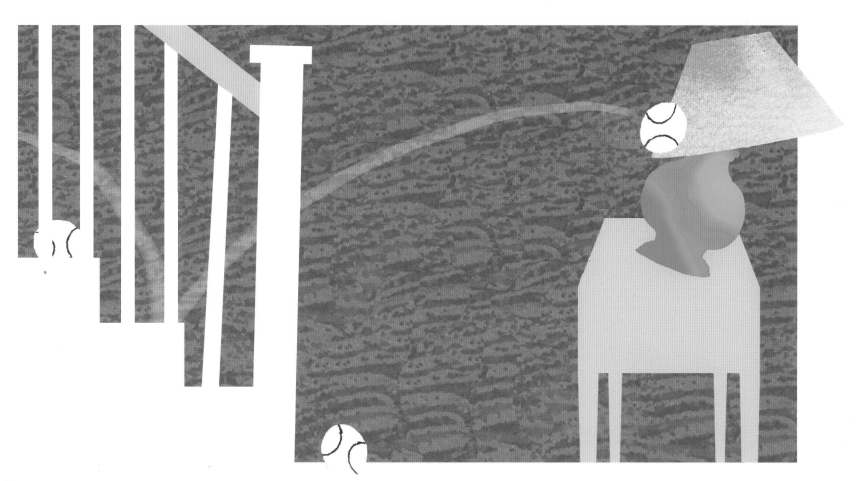

Daddy's grumpy at breakfast because he can't find his newspaper.
I put it where he'd never find it.

"There's no reading the paper
on a Daddy Adventure Day,"
Mommy reminds him.

At the train station my daddy buys a super-jumbo coffee because he's so tired. I get two hot chocolates because I spill the first one on his pants.

"Nobody will even notice," I say.

I tell everybody on the train that my daddy is taking me to my first baseball game ever. Then I catch him talking on his cell phone.

Calling work on a Daddy Adventure Day is not allowed.

I can see our baseball stadium from a few blocks away. It's even taller when we get up close. Baseball is bigger than I thought!

Before we get to our seats, my daddy buys me a hat, a teddy bear wearing a baseball glove, and a pointy flag on a stick.

I always get a lot of great stuff on a Daddy Adventure Day.

It's humongous inside.
There's organ music.
And seagulls.

And more faces than I've ever seen.
The grass looks like a green checkerboard.

"Are you okay?" my daddy keeps asking me.

"I'm just getting used to it," I tell him.

Everybody stands for the national anthem.
I don't know the words, but I sing super loud anyway.
Today we're watching the white shirts play the blue shirts.
"We want the white shirts to win," my daddy tells me.
"C'MON, WHITE SHIRTS! YOU CAN WIN IT!" I scream.
I like the screaming part even more than the singing part.

Soon baseballs
are crashing down
all around us.
    "Those are foul
balls," my daddy
explains.
    "Nobody ever said
anything about *them*,"
I mumble.

When a man one row in front of us catches one, he leans over and hands the ball to me.

He must know a Daddy Adventure Day when he sees one.

When a player hits the ball all the way into the ocean, my daddy throws me up in the air.

"What happened?" I shout.

"That's three runs for the white shirts!" he shouts back.

While we high-five all the people around
us, my root beer spills on Daddy's pants.
   "Now your hot-chocolate
leg won't feel so lonely!"
I say to cheer him up.

We sneak out before the game is over and go to a fancy restaurant because we saved plenty of room for dessert. The waiter brings me a free banana split with extra cherries when he hears that today is a Daddy Adventure Day.

This time I don't spill any on Daddy's pants.

"Who won?" Mommy asks when I open the front door.

"The white shirts, of course," I say. "We whupped 'em!"

I tell Mommy all about the hot chocolate and the banana split with extra cherries.

"You always eat well on a Daddy Adventure Day," Mommy says.

Her eyes get extra big when I show her my foul ball.

"You caught a foul ball at your first baseball game ever?" she says, and whistles.

I just smile.

"What happened to Daddy's pants?"
Mommy laughs.
  "Baseball is messier than you think,"
I say.

Later, me and Daddy lay on the couch watching the baseball
that flew all the way into the ocean. It doesn't look as far on TV.
The grass doesn't look as green either.
Or the ball as white.
And they never even show the seagulls.

But I remember.
You never forget a Daddy Adventure Day.

For my adventurous daughter, Jade, whose trip with her daddy
to her first big-league ballgame inspired this story. —DK

Hail to patient dads everywhere!
And with gratitude to my editor, Michael Green,
and art director, Cecilia Yung, for helping me do my best.
Thank you! —SR

PHILOMEL BOOKS · A division of Penguin Young Readers Group. Published by The Penguin Group.
Penguin Group (USA) Inc., 375 Hudson Street, New York, NY 10014, U.S.A.
Penguin Group (Canada), 90 Eglinton Avenue East, Suite 700, Toronto, Ontario M4P 2Y3, Canada (a division of Pearson Penguin Canada Inc.).
Penguin Books Ltd, 80 Strand, London WC2R 0RL, England.
Penguin Ireland, 25 St. Stephen's Green, Dublin 2, Ireland (a division of Penguin Books Ltd).
Penguin Group (Australia), 250 Camberwell Road, Camberwell, Victoria 3124, Australia (a division of Pearson Australia Group Pty Ltd).
Penguin Books India Pvt Ltd, 11 Community Centre, Panchsheel Park, New Delhi - 110 017, India.
Penguin Group (NZ), 67 Apollo Drive, Rosedale, North Shore 0632, New Zealand (a division of Pearson New Zealand Ltd).
Penguin Books (South Africa) (Pty) Ltd, 24 Sturdee Avenue, Rosebank, Johannesburg 2196, South Africa.
Penguin Books Ltd, Registered Offices: 80 Strand, London WC2R 0RL, England.

Published simultaneously in Canada. Manufactured in China by South China Printing Co. Ltd.
Design by Marikka Tamura. Text set in Triplex Serif. The illustrations in this book are done in watercolor and digital collage.
Library of Congress Cataloging-in-Publication Data
Keane, David, 1965–
Daddy Adventure Day / Dave Keane ; illustrated by Sue Ramá.   p. cm.
Summary: Daddy Adventure Days are always special, and this one, featuring a boy's first visit to a baseball stadium, is no exception.
[1. Fathers and sons—Fiction. 2. Baseball—Fiction.] I. Ramá, Sue, ill. II. Title.   PZ7.K2172Dad 2011   [E]—dc22   2010024077
ISBN 978-0-399-24627-2
10 9 8 7 6 5 4 3 2 1